DISNEY
CLUB PENGUIN™

The
Card-Jitsu™
Handbook

D0111247

by Katherine Noll

Grosset & Dunlap
An Imprint of Penguin Group (USA) Inc.

GROSSET & DUNLAP
Published by the Penguin Group
Penguin Group (USA) Inc., 375 Hudson Street, New York, New York 10014, USA
Penguin Group (Canada), 90 Eglinton Avenue East, Suite 700, Toronto, Ontario
M4P 2Y3, Canada (a division of Pearson Penguin Canada Inc.)
Penguin Books Ltd., 80 Strand, London WC2R 0RL, England
Penguin Group Ireland, 25 St. Stephen's Green, Dublin 2, Ireland
(a division of Penguin Books Ltd.)
Penguin Group (Australia), 250 Camberwell Road, Camberwell, Victoria 3124,
Australia (a division of Pearson Australia Group Pty. Ltd.)
Penguin Books India Pvt. Ltd., 11 Community Centre,
Panchsheel Park, New Delhi–110 017, India
Penguin Group (NZ), 67 Apollo Drive, Rosedale, Auckland 0632, New Zealand
(a division of Pearson New Zealand Ltd.)
Penguin Books (South Africa) (Pty.) Ltd., 24 Sturdee Avenue,
Rosebank, Johannesburg 2196, South Africa

Penguin Books Ltd., Registered Offices: 80 Strand, London WC2R 0RL, England

ISBN 978-0-448-45539-6   10 9 8 7 6 5 4 3 2 1

It started as a myth, born out of the shadows

A mysterious figure appeared to train those who were willing in the ancient art of *Card-Jitsu*. This journey requires patience, practice, and power. Those brave enough to walk the path of the ninja will be tested. Courage is required.

Those who learn to master the ancient art of *Card-Jitsu* will face Sensei in an epic match. It will be unlike anything they have experienced before.

Are you ready to begin your journey? Turn the page.

Walk the Path of the Master

Throughout this book, you'll follow in Sensei's footsteps to learn *Card-Jitsu*. Once you understand the power of fire, water, and snow, you will become a ninja.

Those who are already ninjas will discover tips and secrets to help them with the next steps of their ninja journeys.

Sensei will appear throughout this guide with words of advice. Those ready to walk the path will also have the chance to train with Sensei. He'll challenge your *Card-Jitsu* and ninja skills with a series of challenges throughout the book. You can check your answers on pages 78–80 to see if you've passed his challenges. If at first you don't succeed, try again!

> It matters not if the belt is white or black. Even masters have much to learn.

Only the Determined May Enter

To begin your journey as a ninja, you must find the Dojo. You'll find it on your map, high up in the mountains.

You'll first encounter the peaceful Dojo courtyard. If you look carefully, you'll notice that the Dojo is surrounded by the three elements of *Card-Jitsu*: water, fire, and snow. Water flows from the Waterfall, fire burns deep inside the Volcano, and snow covers the mountainside.

This mysterious place was first discovered after a lightning strike. Penguins helped uncover the hidden building, which had sat empty for a long time.

> Only those who try ever succeed. Those who don't, only they will fail.

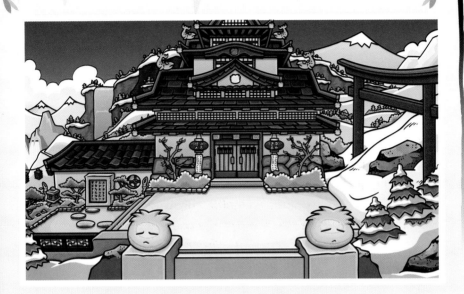

Click on the double doors of the ancient stone building to enter the Dojo. Here you'll start on the path of the ninja, facing challenges and rivals. Look inside yourself for the strength to succeed.

Explore the room. You'll find everything you need to get started on your *Card-Jitsu* journey!

Tips!

- Train with a partner on the practice mats.
- See how you are progressing in your quest to become a ninja.
- Read the instructions to learn how the game is played.
- Have Sensei set you up in matches with other penguins so you can earn your belts.

Sensei's Journey

How did the Dojo come to exist? This is what Sensei had to say:

"One night as I was camping under the stars, I looked to a waterfall and learned a valuable lesson.

River flows here
from the mountaintop
and learns to become waterfall.

'I, too, have come here to learn,' I said out loud. 'Here I will build my dojo.' Then I looked to the snow I stood on and learned a valuable lesson.

See how river leaps
from high snow ledge to snow bed?
New places to learn.

'A dojo must have many places to learn in,' I said out loud. 'I will build strong walls and use rice paper flats to make rooms.' Then I looked at my campfire and saw a valuable lesson there.

But how can you learn
in a dojo without light?
Fire is needed.

'I will carve stone lanterns,' I said out loud. 'So fire can come inside with me.'

Having learned from water, snow, and fire, I built the Dojo in the mountains. When it was finished, I went wandering in the wilderness, learning and seeking wisdom. After lightning struck the Dojo, I appeared on the mountain to let penguins know I had returned. Now I teach the path of the ninja to all those who want to learn."

Become a Master of the Elements: Learn Card-Jitsu

Becoming a ninja takes time. To begin, you must learn how to play *Card-Jitsu* and study the power of the elements.

Element Expert

Card-Jitsu is a card-based game where you battle with the elements of fire, snow, and water. You and your opponent each throw a card. The strongest element wins the match.

 Water puts out fire

 Fire melts snow

 Snow freezes water

If you throw a snow card and your opponent throws a water card, you win the hand. Snow beats water. But if you throw a fire card and your opponent throws a water card, you lose the hand. Water beats fire. The winning card will appear on the screen above you and your opponent.

A journey of a thousand miles begins with a good pair of sneakers.

Number Knowledge

What happens if both you and your opponent play the same element? In that case, the card with the highest number wins. If you play a number six snow card, but your opponent uses a number eight snow card, your opponent wins the hand. If you both play a card of the same element and the same number, the match is a tie and the battle continues.

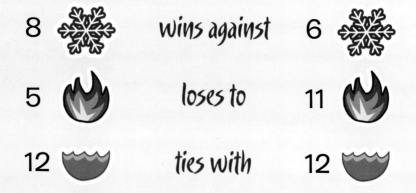

8 ❄ wins against 6 ❄

5 🔥 loses to 11 🔥

12 💧 ties with 12 💧

Circle the card that would win each match.

1.

2.

3.

4.

Check page 78 to see if you're right!

Winning a Match

There are two ways you can win a *Card-Jitsu* battle. The first way is by having one card of each element in different colors. (Each card has a color border around it—red, purple, blue, yellow, green, or orange.)

The second is by having three cards of the same element in different colors.

Tip!

When playing online, if you forget how you can win a game, place your cursor over the question mark in the middle of the screen and you'll get a reminder.

Know Your Power Cards

When certain cards are played, they'll change the rules for the next hand. These are called Power Cards. The borders of these cards will glow when they appear on your screen. Place your cursor over the card to read the new rule. That way, you'll know when it is best to use the card and the best move to make on your next turn. If your opponent plays a Power Card and wins the hand, look for a symbol at the top of your screen that will show you the rule change.

One of the game changers you'll see a lot is this:

It means that lower-numbered cards of the same element will win that hand instead of the higher numbers. So if  is in play, which card would win?

The number six fire card would win, but only for that hand.

White Belt Challenge

Greetings, Grasshopper. I see you have been learning the ancient art of *Card-Jitsu*. Just like the pebbles of a riverbed that steer the rapids toward the sea, I must guide you into becoming the best *Card-Jitsu* player you can be. That is why it is now time for a test! Ha-ha. Do not look so nervous, Grasshopper. We will start small like the seed that has the potential to grow into the mighty oak.

You and your opponent have each picked a card to play. Which card wins the hand? Put a check in the Win column if your card has won or a check in the Try Again column if your opponent has won.

YOU	YOUR OPPONENT	WIN	TRY AGAIN

YOU	YOUR OPPONENT	WIN	TRY AGAIN
❄ 11	👑 10		
🔥 2 → 9 7	🔥 5		
❄ 9	🔥 2		
❄ 6	👑 12		
❄ 3 → 9 7	❄ 11		
🔥 6	👑 8		
❄ 4	🔥 11		

Check page 78 to see if you're right!

Wear Your Belt Proudly

They are not sold in the Gift Shop. You cannot find them as free items at the latest Club Penguin party. The only way to get a *Card-Jitsu* belt is to earn one through hard work and dedication. You'll see ninjas-in-training wearing their belts with pride all over the island.

Every time you play a match or practice *Card-Jitsu*, you get a little closer to earning a new belt. Here are all the belts you can obtain on your journey to becoming a ninja.

And though we wear our belts and show our ranks proudly when we stand. When we sit together, we are equals.

Yellow Belt Challenge

Yellow Belt Challenge

We meet again, Grasshopper. Was that last test challenging enough for you? Oh, but your training has only begun, and I can sense that you are ready for even more! Ninjas can find their way anywhere and have a great sense of direction. Now I will challenge your ability to find your way through a maze of snow, water, and fire obstacles. Focus, my student, and hone your skills!

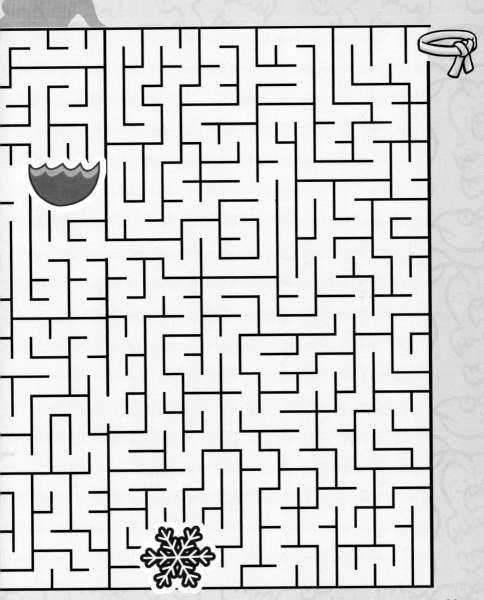

Check page 78 to see if you're right!

Are You Ready?

When you visit the Dojo, you have two options. You can play a practice match or have Sensei find an opponent for you to battle.

Practice Makes Perfect

If you want to practice before competing against another ninja-in-training, head over to one of the blue practice mats in the Dojo. You'll have to wait until another penguin comes to the mat you are on before you can begin. To challenge a buddy to *Card-Jitsu*, go to the same mat together. Practicing does help you earn belts. However, you'll earn belts faster if you ask Sensei to match you with an opponent.

Talk to Sensei

To get started, talk to Sensei. He will sometimes appear out of thin air in a puff of smoke, sitting on a pillow in the corner of the Dojo. Sensei will set you up in matches with other penguins so you can earn your belts. You can battle Sensei at any time, but you won't have a chance to challenge him until you've earned your black belt.

Sensei will try to match you with a student with similar abilities. If you are a white belt, he'll try to find another white belt for you to battle. But sometimes a white belt may face a black belt in a *Card-Jitsu* match. If that happens to you, don't give up. Every match gives you the chance to learn and grow.

Nobody trips over mountains. It is the small pebble that causes you to stumble. Go one pebble at a time, and soon you will have climbed the entire mountain.

25

Battle with Honor

Each *Card-Jitsu* match begins and ends with the players bowing to each other. It's a sign of respect for the game and your opponent. If you are losing a battle, don't leave the match before it is finished. Finish every game you start. Even losing a *Card-Jitsu* match helps you earn points toward a belt.

If you win a match, don't tease or rub it in to your opponent. And if you lose, don't get angry at the winner. You and your fellow ninjas-in-training are all working toward the same goal. Make Sensei proud!

Like the great cookie, we must have honor, strength . . . and chocolate chips.

Orange Belt Challenge

Orange Belt Challenge

Good day, my student. I see you have found your way through the maze. Well done! I am pleased that like the buzzing mosquito, you do not give up, no matter how many flippers may swat at you.

Student, never forget that a ninja is always a ninja. It matters not if you are in the Dojo or in your igloo. Always behave with honor. Think like a ninja when you answer the questions below. Good luck, my student!

What Would a Ninja Do?

1. Becoming a ninja is not easy. A new *Card-Jitsu* player asks for some help learning the game. A ninja would:
A) say "Good luck, you'll need it."
B) ignore the penguin
C) offer to train with the penguin

2. Ninjas like to dance, too! While dancing with buddies at the Night Club, a ninja notices a shy penguin watching but not joining in. A ninja would:
A) keep dancing
B) throw a snowball at the penguin
C) invite the penguin to dance

3. There's a cave-in in the Mine Shack. Construction workers are needed fast! A ninja would:
A) grab a jackhammer and start drilling
B) head to the Dojo for training
C) play a game instead

4. It's time to find the newest pin! A penguin who is new to the island is asking other penguins for help. A ninja would:
A) get mad at the penguins who don't answer
B) help the new penguin find the pin
C) tell the new penguin to figure it out on his or her own

5. *Puffle Rescue* is a fun game. But getting past all those sharks is tough! The ninja would:
A) give up
B) keep trying
C) look for a way to cheat

6. Time to redecorate! A ninja wants a new look for his igloo. He or she would choose:
A) a dojo theme
B) a gym theme
C) anything the ninja wanted—ninjas are all individuals with their own unique personalities!

7. Walking through town, a ninja notices a group of penguins teasing another penguin. The ninja would:
A) yell at the group of penguins
B) join the group of penguins and start teasing, too
C) ask the penguin being teased to play a game

8. Keeping Club Penguin safe is important to ninjas. After hearing about a classified secret agency on the island that does just that, a ninja would:
A) help keep Club Penguin safe by joining the Elite Penguin Force
B) think that he or she cannot be both a secret agent and a ninja. Penguins are only allowed to be one or the other.
C) think it might be too hard to be a secret agent and not try

Check page 78 to see if you're right!

Which Element Are You?

Ninjas use the heat of fire, the iciness of snow, and the rush of water against their opponents. While ninjas must master all the elements, some might notice they are more in tune with one element than another. Which element are you most like?

1. **Let's start simply. Pick which color you like best.**
   A) red
   B) blue
   C) white

2. **When you get mad:**
   A) You yell so everyone knows it!
   B) You talk about how you're feeling.
   C) You keep it to yourself.

3. **Your favorite kind of day is:**
   A) hot, hot, hot!
   B) rainy
   C) snowy

4. **In a crowd of people, you:**
   A) like to be the center of attention
   B) talk to someone new—maybe you'll make a new friend
   C) feel shy

5. **If you could choose an exotic pet, you would pick a:**
   A) dragon
   B) shark
   C) polar bear

6. **A fun way to get around would be on:**
   A) an airplane
   B) a cruise ship
   C) a snowmobile

Give yourself one point for each *A*, two points for each *B*, and three points for each *C*.

What's Your Total?

 8-13: Fire—You are not afraid to take chances during a match. Your bold style can surprise your opponents and give you big wins. But sometimes you lose big, too. That's okay. You wouldn't want it any other way!

 14-19: Water—You often rely on intuition when choosing a card, leaving your opponents wondering if you can read their minds! Remember to trust your instincts, and you'll be a ninja in no time.

 20-24: Snow—You carefully consider all scenarios before your next move. Your thoughtful *Card-Jitsu* style makes you a tough player to beat.

Green Belt Challenge

Hello again, my student. I am very proud of you. You are quickly on your way to becoming a ninja—but not so fast! Many more trials lie ahead. Now that you know what a ninja would do, do you know where a ninja would hide? It is easy for a ninja to win hide-and-seek, even without disappearing. Ha-ha! Look at the picture below and try to find the ninja. Stay focused, Grasshopper!

Check page 78 to see if you're right!

Mastering Card-Jitsu

The basics of *Card-Jitsu* are simple: Water puts out fire, fire melts snow, snow freezes water. But as you train, you'll discover there is more to it than meets the eye. You can predict what card your opponent might play based on what they need to win and make your moves based on this prediction.

For example, your opponent needs a fire card to win the game. If you think she might play a fire card, you could play a water card to beat her.

Your opponent needs a water card to win.
Snow freezes water, so try a snow card.

Your opponent needs a snow card to win.
Fire melts snow, so try a fire card.

However, in the last example, if your opponent is a skilled *Card-Jitsu* player, she might guess that you will play a fire card to beat her snow card. She may then instead play a water card to beat your fire card.

Running through different scenarios may seem difficult at first, but the more you practice, the better you'll get at it. Remember, there is no foolproof way to predict which card your opponent will play. You can only make your best guess based on your cards, your opponent, and what your opponent needs to win.

A bird in the hand makes it hard to eat pizza.

Blue Belt Challenge

Blue Belt Challenge

Good work, Grasshopper. Like the mighty earthquake, you have rocked the house! This next challenge will be tougher than the last—but remember, it does not matter how slowly you go as long as you don't stop. Carefully examine who your opponent is and which card they need to win. Write in your answer using all the knowledge you have learned. Remember, nothing is certain in *Card-Jitsu*. Cards can change like the seasons. Try your best, and you will have already won.

YOUR OPPONENT	OPPONENT NEEDS THIS ELEMENT TO WIN	YOU PLAY

YOUR OPPONENT	OPPONENT NEEDS THIS ELEMENT TO WIN	YOU PLAY

Check page 79 to see if you're right!

Putting the Cards in Card-Jitsu

The first time you visit the Dojo and speak with Sensei, he gives you a starter pack of cards to use during your *Card-Jitsu* matches.

The starter deck has nine cards (three for each element) and comes with a Power Card. Whenever a player wins a battle with a Power Card, you'll see that move in action. Whether it's a penguin squirting hot sauce or throwing a snowball or water balloon, watching what happens is as fun as playing *Card-Jitsu* itself.

Tip!

You can buy *Card-Jitsu* cards to add to your collection! These new cards will help you earn belts faster! Turn to page 48 for more information about taking the Fast Path!

An apple a day keeps the doctor away. But never changing your socks keeps everyone away!

Red Belt Challenge

Red Belt Challenge

I am impressed, my student! Just like the rapid current of the mighty river, you are moving forward with ease. You have come this far, so I am confident you will pass this next test easily. Have you been paying attention? I hope so. After all, the best way to keep good acts in your memory is to repeat them. See if you can remember and repeat what you have learned so far.

1. Where was the Dojo found?
A) the Iceberg
B) the mountains
C) the Forest

2. The Dojo is surrounded by the three elements of *Card-Jitsu*.
A) true
B) false

3. Which of the following is NOT an element used in *Card-Jitsu*?
A) fire
B) water
C) wind

4. Sensei came up with the idea to build the Dojo while he was
A) camping under the stars
B) playing *Card-Jitsu*
C) drinking tea

5. A bird in the hand makes it hard to
A) play *Card-Jitsu*
B) eat pizza
C) play the piano

6. The first belt a ninja trainee can earn is
A) white
B) orange
C) purple

7. Each *Card-Jitsu* match begins and ends with:
A) Sensei ringing a gong
B) the Hokey Pokey
C) the players bowing to each other

8. When you see (9 / 1) during *Card-Jitsu*, it means:
A) lower-numbered cards are worth more than higher-numbered cards
B) you can add two points to whatever card you play in the next round
C) you have to do ninety-one push-ups

9. Special cards that change the rules for the next hand are called:
A) Fire Cards
B) Power Cards
C) Ninja Cards

10. Once you become an experienced *Card-Jitsu* player, you can try to predict which card your opponent will play.
A) true
B) false

Check page 79 to see if you're right!

Taking the Fast Path

Card-Jitsu cards are available for you to collect off-line. Once you get your cards, you can unlock them online, add them to your starter deck, and use them when you play *Card-Jitsu*. Doing this is called the Fast Path because it helps you become a ninja more quickly.

The cards found off-line contain exclusive Power Cards that can give you an edge in battle. Yet you don't need anything but the starter deck to become a ninja. Many penguins have used the starter deck alone to earn their belts and defeat Sensei.

To this day, I still train to get better.

Here are some of the many cool Power Cards that are available.

All Washed Up

Facing these water Power Cards is not easy. In fact, you might end up all wet!

When you play this card and win, Gary the Gadget Guy appears and tests out his new thingamajig. It sets in motion a series of events that ends with a bucket of water falling on your opponent. Scoring with this card will add two points to whatever card you play in the next round.

You can lead a penguin to water, but you can't make him surf.

Win the round with this card, and Alaska, Yukon, and the Golden Puffle will run across the screen. A boulder is chasing them! Luckily, it misses you but chases your opponent away. Your opponent won't be able to play any fire cards on the next turn.

Fired Up

Feel the burn! You'll want to chill out big time if you have to deal with these fire Power Cards.

Win with this card, and you'll meet Herbert P. Bear and Klutzy the Crab! The two will drill a hole in the floor. Your opponent will fall into it. You can discard one of your opponent's orange cards.

You should only fight fire with fire after you have run out of water.

Win with this card, and you'll hand your opponent a cupcake. Sounds sweet, right? Until a fire ninja shows up with a bottle of hot sauce! The ninja drops the hot sauce and gobbles up the cupcake instead. You can discard one of your opponent's snow cards.

Snowed In

Bundle up! When these snow Power Cards are around, the forecast calls for a blizzard.

Win a round with this card, and your opponent is in for a stampede—a puffle stampede! Puffles will swarm over your opponent, and then you can discard one of his or her water cards.

If you defeat your opponent with this card, Shadow Guy and Gamma Gal appear and fire lightning bolts at your opponent until he or she runs away. Scoring with this card will add two points to whatever card you play in the next round.

Purple Belt Challenge

Purple Belt Challenge

Grasshopper, you are even closer to becoming a ninja now. This next challenge is tricky, even for me, so stay alert. You must color in the puffles, so that yellow, red, purple, green, blue, and pink puffles appear once in each row, column, and 3 x 2 box. Take your time, and use logic and the process of elimination to succeed. Remember, every puffle has its day. Ha-ha.

Each puffle color should show up only once in each row.

Each puffle color should show up only once in each box.

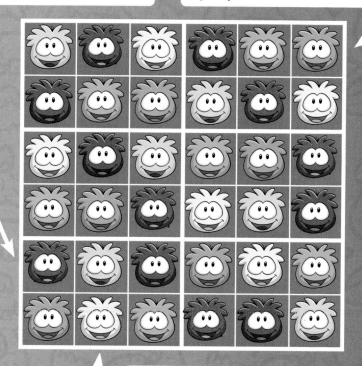

Each puffle color should show up only once in each column.

Think you've got the idea? Give it a try.

Check page 79 to see if you're right!

57

Only a Chosen Few May Enter

Many want to come inside. But only those who have defeated Sensei at *Card-Jitsu* and earned the title of ninja can gain access to the Ninja Hideout.

> The doors of wisdom are never shut.

Once you become a ninja, walk to the stone wall to the left of the main Dojo entrance. The door will open to reveal the secret entrance to the Ninja Hideout. Here you can play *Card-Jitsu* with other black belts and purchase special gear for ninjas and members only. It is also where the next phase of your journey begins as you learn how to master the elements.

Flying Flippers Emporium

You've worked hard to become a ninja. Now you can celebrate by shopping for exclusive items at the Flying Flippers Emporium. From stealthy outfits to Dojo décor, these items are available to ninjas only.

Ninja Outfit

Are the rumors true? Do ninjas really have the ability to become invisible? Buy the ninja outfit and ninja mask and put them on. Then dance and see what happens.

Cloud Wave Bracers

Put these on with your ninja outfit and wave. Where did you go? Only the clouds know.

Hand Gong

Wave to sound the gong.

To dance or wave, click on your toolbar.

Goldsmith Apron

Dance while wearing the apron to use the golden anvil.

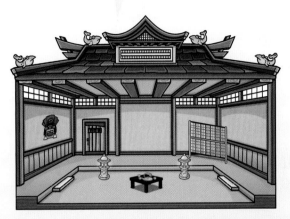

Dojo, Sweet Dojo

You can learn from Sensei's tale of fire, water, and snow and build your own dojo with these items.

The Journey Continues

What new adventures await you as a ninja? If you purchase the amulet, it will unlock hidden doors so you can become a master of the elements.

Stamp of Approval

Did you know that ninjas-in-training can get Stamps by playing *Card-Jitsu*?

> When the pupil is ready, the teacher will come.

To find your Stamp Book, open up your player card and you'll see ⬡. Click it to view your Stamp Book. Use this chart to keep track of the *Card-Jitsu* Stamps you can earn.

STAMP	DESCRIPTION	DIFFICULTY	DATE EARNED
Grasshopper	Begin your journey. Earn your white belt.	Easy	
Fine Student	Reach halfway. Earn your blue belt.	Medium	

STAMP	DESCRIPTION	DIFFICULTY	DATE EARNED
True Ninja	Prove your ninja skills. Earn your black belt.	Hard	
Ninja Master	Defeat Sensei and become a Ninja.	Hard	
Flawless Victory	Win without letting your opponent gain any cards.	Medium	
Match Master	Win twenty-five matches.	Hard	
Elemental Win	Win a match with three different elements.	Easy	

STAMP	DESCRIPTION	DIFFICULTY	DATE EARNED
One Element	Win a match with three cards of the same element.	Medium	
Sensei Card	See the Sensei Power Card.	Extreme	
Full Dojo	Score nine cards before you win.	Extreme	

If you've already done what it takes to earn the Stamps before they were released, don't worry. You can still collect the Stamps. Go back to the Dojo and play a game of *Card-Jitsu*. You'll be awarded any Stamps that you may have already earned.

If you train today, you will be ready for tomorrow.

Brown Belt Challenge

Brown Belt Challenge

You've come quite far, my student! You have bravely faced all the trials you have been given. Are you now ready for the next challenge? A ninja must be able to tackle any puzzle he or she is faced with—even if that puzzle is a haiku. I will recite some haikus for you. All of them will describe something on Club Penguin—can you tell what (or who) each haiku is about?

1.
Take a fun wild ride
when you climb into my cart.
Try not to wipe out.

2.
Is it a rumor?
Or a myth? To find out if
it's true, try to tip!

3.
I have a pink hat.
I write for the *Penguin Times*.
Ask me anything.

4.
He is red and small.
He has very strong pincers.
His friend is a bear.

1.
_____

2.
_____

3.
_____

4.
_____

5.
Shelter inside me.
You can change me anytime.
All you need are coins.

6.
In a ship I sail,
drinkin' drums o' cream soda
with my first mate, Yarr.

7.
I'm always smiling.
You might call me Mix Master.
I love the Night Club.

8.
If my walls could talk
they would speak of fairies, bugs,
vikings, and mermaids.

9.
Fire, water, and ice.
Their power lies within me.
Penguins collect me.

10.
I hide out of sight.
Some might say invisible.
I dress in all black.

5.

6.

7.

8.

9.

10.

Check page 80 to see if you're right!

It's Time

You've visited the Dojo every day, playing match after match.
You've won some; you've lost some. You've patiently worked
toward each belt, starting with the thrill of winning your very
first one until the unforgettable day you earned your black belt.
With pride you wear it, yet your journey is not over. There is still
a goal you must obtain. It is the honor of being called a ninja.
And there's only one way to earn it: Face Sensei himself in a
Card-Jitsu battle.

Earn your belts
Challenge Sensei
Instructions

Getting Ready

What can you do to prepare for your match with Sensei? Actually, you've already done everything you can. By working so hard toward becoming a black belt, you have proven yourself worthy of facing Sensei in battle. When you're ready to challenge Sensei, click on him in the Dojo just like you would for any other match. This time choose "Challenge Sensei."

When you're a black belt,
you must challenge me and win.
And I'm pretty good.

Tips for Battling Sensei

Never give up.

Don't give up.

Seriously, never give up!

No one has beaten Sensei on the first try. In fact, some ninjas have reported challenging Sensei over ten times before they were victorious! If at first you don't win, try again. And again. And again. If you keep at it, you have a good chance of becoming a ninja.

Black Belt Challenge

Black Belt Challenge

My student, I sense power and determination in you. And, like the giant Iceberg, you are pretty cool! Take your time with this test, stay focused, and you will surely taste victory. Good luck, Grasshopper, and may the power of water, snow, and fire be with you as you walk the path of the ninja.

Who wins?

VS.

Who/What am I?

What's that yummy smell?
Penguins flock to this hangout.
I'll take mine with squid.

What should you play?

 needs to win

Fill in the board so the yellow, red, purple, and green puffles appear only once in each row, column, and 2×2 box.

You are winning a *Card-Jitsu* match when your opponent quits the game. What should you do?

A) Find the penguin and yell at him.
B) Report him to a moderator.
C) Ask Sensei to match you with another player and start over.

Who wins?

You have just won the previous round of *Card-Jitsu* with this Power Card. In this round, you played a **6** 🔥 **card** and your opponent played a **7** 🔥 **card**.

Who/What am I?

High in the mountains, a place of learning exists. Here you'll find wisdom.

Check page 80 to see if you're right!

73

Ninja Training

Once you're a ninja, you've got to keep your skills sharp. Here are some things you can do every day to stay worthy of the title of ninja.

To find true wisdom
you must train hard and focus,
and don't skip breakfast.

STEP 1: EAT BREAKFAST

Don't skip the most important meal of the day! Studies show that ninjas who eat breakfast win more matches than those who don't.

STEP 2: FOCUS

Nature has much to teach us about the ways of the ninja. Practice clearing your mind by sitting outside. Close your eyes—what do you hear? Breathe in. What do you smell? Open your eyes and observe a blade of grass or a leaf. What do you see? Doing this will sharpen your mind and your senses.

STEP 3: BE INVISIBLE

Ninjas are known for their stealth. Practice your skills by playing hide-and-seek in the dark. Train yourself to walk quietly so no one can hear you coming.

STEP 4: EXERCISE

Ninjas need to be strong, fast, and flexible. Simple games like tag and playing ball can help with that.

STEP 5: PRACTICE *CARD-JITSU*

If you fail to practice what you learn, the knowledge will disappear.

STEP 6: BE KIND

To be a ninja means to act with a strict code of honor. Help out your friends and family. Strive to be kind to all you meet.

STEP 7: BE SMART

Read a book (like you're doing right now!). Smart ninjas know that a little knowledge goes a long way. Always be open to learning something new. You never know when it will come in handy!

STEP 8: EAT HEALTHY

Your body is a machine that needs good fuel in order to run well. Since ninjas need to be in tip-top shape, when you can, try to choose healthy snacks like fruits and vegetables.

STEP 9: GET ENOUGH SLEEP

How are you going to harness the power of fire, water, and snow if you are sleepy? Make sure to be in bed early every night to recharge those ninja batteries.

The Journey Is Just Beginning

Once you become a ninja, your *Card-Jitsu* experience is not over. In fact, your journey is just beginning! More intense training awaits. Sensei will guide you to become a master of fire, water, and snow. Always look to the mountains and watch for signs. Keep practicing and be ready.

SENSEI VANISH!

Answer Key

Pages 12-13
NUMBER KNOWLEDGE
1. number eight water card
2. number six water card
3. number seven snow card
4. number two fire card

Pages 18-19
WHITE BELT CHALLENGE
FIRST ROW: Win
SECOND ROW: Try Again
THIRD ROW: Win
FOURTH ROW: Win
FIFTH ROW: Win
SIXTH ROW: Try Again
SEVENTH ROW: Win
EIGHTH ROW: Win
NINTH ROW: Try Again
TENTH ROW: Try Again

Pages 22-23
YELLOW BELT CHALLENGE

Pages 28-29
ORANGE BELT CHALLENGE
1. C
2. C
3. A
4. B
5. B
6. C
7. C
8. A

Pages 34-35
GREEN BELT CHALLENGE

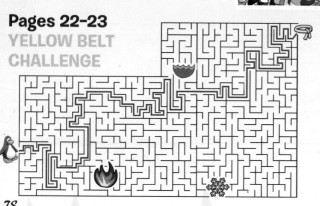

Pages 40–41
BLUE BELT CHALLENGE

FIRST ROW: Your opponent played a snow card. If you played a fire card, you won!

SECOND ROW: Your opponent played a fire card. If you played a water card, you won!

THIRD ROW: Your opponent played a water card. If you played a snow card, you won!

FOURTH ROW: Your opponent played a fire card. If you played a water card, you won!

FIFTH ROW: Your opponent played a water card. If you played a snow card, you won!

SIXTH ROW: Your opponent played a snow card. If you played a fire card, you won!

SEVENTH ROW: Your opponent played a water card. If you played a snow card, you won!

EIGHTH ROW: Your opponent played a snow card. If you played a fire card, you won!

NINTH ROW: Your opponent played a fire card. If you played a water card, you won!

TENTH ROW: Your opponent played a fire card. If you played a water card, you won!

Pages 46–47
RED BELT CHALLENGE

1. B
2. A
3. C
4. A
5. Ha-ha! My little joke. While I did say B, I will accept any answer for this question.
6. A
7. C
8. A
9. B
10. A

Pages 56–57
PURPLE BELT CHALLENGE

Pages 66-67
BROWN BELT CHALLENGE

1. *Cart Surfer*
2. Iceberg
3. Aunt Arctic
4. Klutzy the Crab
5. Igloo
6. Captain Rockhopper
7. Cadence
8. The Stage
9. *Card-Jitsu* cards
10. Ninja

Page 76
THE JOURNEY IS JUST BEGINNING

Ha-ha! You found me! But did you find the ninjas? There are eleven ninjas hiding in the pages of this book. See if you can find them, Grasshopper.

Pages 72-73
BLACK BELT CHALLENGE

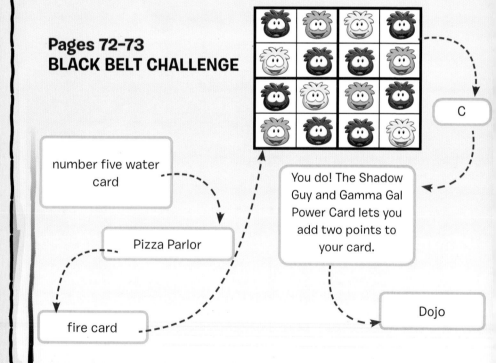

number five water card

C

Pizza Parlor

You do! The Shadow Guy and Gamma Gal Power Card lets you add two points to your card.

fire card

Dojo